The Tower

A Story of Humility

BY RICHARD PAUL EVANS

ILLUSTRATIONS BY JONATHAN LINTON

Simon & Schuster Books for Young Readers
NEW YORK LONDON TORONTO SYDNEY SINGAPORE

ARTIST'S AKNOWLEDGMENTS

I wish to thank Alice, Mel, Ciming, Libo, Minhua, Tong, Jian, Cissy, Hannah, Yongfang, and especially Richard Chang, for being such great models. Thanks also go to Rick and his wonderful staff for their friendship, ideas, and talents; and to Ann Brashares, Russell Gordon, Steve Geck, and the many others, without whom there would be no book. I want to thank my wife—my love and inspiration—and everyone in my family for their support and encouragement. And mostly I thank God and His Son, who live to bless and lift each one of us.

—J. M. L.

SIMON & SCHUSTER BOOKS FOR YOUNG READERS
An imprint of Simon & Schuster Children's Publishing Division
1230 Avenue of the Americas, New York, New York 10020
Text copyright © 2001 by Richard Paul Evans
Illustrations copyright © 2001 by Jonathan Linton
The text of this book is set in 15-pt. Weiss.
The illustrations are rendered in oil paint.
Printed in the United States of America
2 4 6 8 10 9 7 5 3 1

Library of Congress Cataloging-in-Publication Data

Evans, Richard Paul.
The tower : a story of humility / by Richard Paul Evans ; illustrated by Jonathan Linton.
p. cm.
Summary: A young man who desires to be great builds a tower higher than any pagoda so that people will look up to him.
ISBN 0-689-83467-5
[1. Pride and vanity—Fiction. 2. Conduct of life—Fiction.] I. Linton, Jonathan, ill. II. Title.
PZ7.E89227 To 2001
[Fic]—dc21
2001040071

Produced by 17th Street Productions,
an Alloy Online, Inc. company
151 West 26th Street, New York, NY 10001

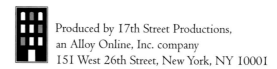

To McKenna

—R. P. E.

To all who love others as themselves

—J. M. L.

*T*here was once a young man who desired to be great. But he did not know how to become great. So he went to the oldest man in the small village where he lived, for all trusted the old man and considered him wise.

"What is it to be great?" the young man asked.

"To be great is to be looked up to," said the old man.

The young man considered his words. Then he went home and built himself a platform to stand on. He took his platform to the center of the village and stood on it. "Now everyone must look up to me."

But not everyone did. That afternoon a very tall man walked by.

"I must build a taller platform," he said. He sawed off a bamboo pole and added longer legs to his platform. Now he could see the top of the villagers' heads. "Now I am greater than they," he said, looking down on the people. "They all must look up to me."

"Not I," said a small voice.

He glanced around. A little girl stared down at him from the window of a pagoda.

"This will not do," said the young man. "What I need is a tower. A tower higher than anything ever built in this village."

He went to work building his tower. He chopped down an entire forest of trees and dragged them to the top of a hill. He worked long and hard every day, from sunrise to late into the night. He did not have time for family or friends or sunset walks along the banks of the river. Whenever someone approached him, he said, "Do not bother me. I am building a tower." Eventually everyone stayed away.

After many seasons the young man finished his tower. It stretched high into the air, high above the village. It was taller than the Pagoda of Dragons, higher even than the emperor's palace in the land to the north. The young man was tired, but he was pleased with his tower. "Now everyone must look up to me," he said. "I am the greatest man in the land."

There was room for only one at the top of his tower, and the young man soon found that he was lonely. But he told himself that it did not matter, for a great man must often walk alone. Besides, he reasoned, why would he want to associate with those so much lower than himself?

One day a bird flying by saw the young man on top of the tower. It flew down and lit on his knee. "What are you doing up here?" the bird asked.

Normally the young man would have sent away such a common bird, but today he was feeling especially lonely and welcomed its company. "I am a great man," he said.

"Is that so?" said the bird. "A great man is an uncommon and good thing. I have always wanted to see a great man. Let me take a look at you."

The bird flew around the man. Then it landed again on the young man's knee. "Excuse me for saying so, but I do not see anything about you that is so different from any other man. What makes you great?" the bird asked.

The young man smiled smugly. He did not expect a bird to know such things as what makes a man great. "Let me explain," he said. "I am much higher than everyone else. All must look up to me." He pointed to the people in the village below. "See how small they are from here."

"It would appear so," said the bird. "But then, perhaps, from the ground, you appear small to them."

For a moment the man puzzled, then he said, "No matter. I am above them all. While they crawl with the animals and work their low fields, I sit high above them in the clouds."

"You are high indeed," said the bird. "It is a long way to fall."

"I will not fall," said the man. "My tower is strong, the likes of which has never been seen in this kingdom."

"All towers fall," said the bird, "with time."

The man ignored the bird's warning. He thought himself much too great to heed a common bird.

"You may be as great as you say," said the bird, "but I know of one who is greater."

The man cast his eyes about. "Where is this person?"

"She is an old woman. She is far below. She could never climb such a tower," said the bird, "but even we birds look up to her."

An arrogant grin crossed the man's face. "I have caught you in foolishness. If she is down below, how can she be looked up to?"

"I cannot explain it, but it is true," said the bird.

This angered the young man. "Where will I find this woman?"

"Where the river is at its widest, there is a large rock just right for sitting upon. At sunrise you will find her there." With that the bird flew away.

The bird's words bothered the man. He decided that he must see this woman for himself. He woke very early the next morning. Before the sun rose above the eastern mountains, he climbed down from his tower. At sunrise he found the woman where the bird said she would be. To his surprise she was a very small woman, old and withered. Her clothes were ragged and poor. Still, she was surrounded by flocks of birds, for she took from her own loaf of bread and fed them.

"I have heard that you are great," the man said to the old woman.

The old woman looked up, but did not reply. She broke off another piece of her bread and threw it to the ground.

"You cannot be great," said the man. "No one looks up to you . . . except these little birds."

"No matter," the old woman replied.

The man puffed out his chest. "What do you know of the great man on the tower? You know of him, of course."

"All know of him," said the woman. "Whether he be great or not I know not. He is nothing to me. But I pity him."

"Pity!" cried the man. "How can you pity a man whom all look up to?"

"I pity him because I think he must be miserable. He spends his life where it is cold and friendless. It is my experience that those who build such towers do not enjoy the climb or the height, but only to be higher than another. Such people must always be lonely."

The man replied tersely, "It is a small price to pay for being great."

"How do you know that the man is great?" she asked.

"Because all can see him and that makes him great."

"Being seen and being great are not the same thing."

"I don't understand," said the man.

"To be great," said the woman, "is not to be seen by, but to truly see, others."

The woman threw the last of her bread to the birds, then turned and faced the man. "To be great is not to be higher than another, but to lift another higher."

The man thought long and hard about this. "You speak strange things."

"Perhaps. But I am too old to lie."

The man turned and walked back to his tower. As he walked he came to a group of children playing. From his tower he could not hear the laughter of children, so he stopped to listen to it. Then he noticed a little boy sitting on the branch of a tree, apart from the others. The boy looked sad.

"Why are you not playing with the others?" the man asked.

"I would rather sit above them in this tree," he replied.

"But why?"

"Because it is better to be above them." He pointed toward the man's tower. "Someday I will build a tower like the one on the hill. Then I will be happy."

"No," said the man as he turned to leave. "You will not be happy then."

The man walked slowly back to his tower and looked at it for a long time. It stretched high up to the cold and lonely clouds. He thought about the old woman and the things she had said. And he thought about the little boy in the tree.

Then he took an axe and began to chop at the legs of the tower. To his surprise the tower fell easily with a mighty crash. The man sat down on a rock to think.

A villager was walking by and stopped to look at the man and the large pile of tangled wood behind him. "I am newly married and hope to build my wife a house. I could use some wood," he said.

"Help yourself to it," the man said.

The new husband began to gather the wood.

"Do you need some help building?" the man asked. "I have gotten good at building."

The husband smiled. "Thank you. I could use some help."

Word of the fallen tower spread throughout the village. There were many in need of wood, and the man shared freely of his tower with all who asked, turning no one away. Some used the wood to build fires to warm themselves and their families. Some made beautiful furniture and carvings. The man even helped a group build a school in the center of the village. The whole village was changed by his gift.

As the man delivered up the last of his wood, he overheard one villager say to another, "Look how freely this man gives. You know what they say of him?"

"What is that?" asked the other.

"It is said that here is a truly great man."

What is the most important thing
we can do for our at-risk children?

In 1996, Richard and Keri Evans sponsored a children's welfare conference to discuss this question. The answer was to create The Christmas Box House International, an organization dedicated to helping abused and neglected children by building special shelter/assessment facilities. The Christmas Box House is a one-stop shelter and assessment facility for abused and neglected children—children who are currently shuffled from agency to agency, from police officer to doctor to caseworker, before being thrust into a new home. At The Christmas Box House all these visits occur on-site, providing familiarity and comfort at a difficult time. In addition, The Christmas Box House brings together child advocates, including foster families, Children's Advocacy Centers, the Center for Children's Justice, and government agencies, to provide and enhance services for at-risk children.

For more information about The Christmas Box House, or to make a contribution, please visit our Web site at:

www.richardpaulevans.com

or write to us at:

Richard Paul Evans
P.O. Box 1416
Salt Lake City, Utah 84110